For my daughter, Jenny,
and her Grandpa, Charles,
with much love

E.D.

For Grandpa Joe and Nan Winnie,
who I know will be smiling down at
the catastrophe that this cake is

G.R.

This edition published by Parragon Books Ltd in 2014 and distributed by
Parragon Inc.
440 Park Avenue South, 13th Floor
New York, NY 10016
www.parragon.com

Published by arrangement with Gullane Children's Books

Text © Elizabeth Dale 2012
Illustrations © Gemma Raynor 2012

ISBN 978-1-4723-3759-7

Printed in China

The Carrot Cake Catastrophe!

Elizabeth Dale

illustrated by

Gemma Raynor

PaRragon

Bath • New York • Singapore • Hong Kong • Cologne • Delhi
Melbourne • Amsterdam • Johannesburg • Shenzhen

Jenny was very excited.
Today was her mommy's birthday and, while she was out,
Jenny and Grandpa were planning a birthday surprise.

"Let's make
a carrot cake!"

cried Jenny.

They found a carrot cake recipe in
Mommy's recipe book. It looked delicious.

"Can you read the big words for me, Grandpa?" asked Jenny.
Grandpa put on his glasses, the kind that made writing clear,
but everything else kind of **blurry**.

"Two-thirds of a cup of **butter**," he read.

He peered around.
"Now, where's that butter...?"

"What's next?" asked Jenny, scooping it into the bowl.

"One and a quarter cups of **flour**," read Grandpa.

OH, NO! Grandpa grabbed…

...the powdered sugar!

White clouds flew everywhere.
"**Oops!**" giggled Jenny.

Once Grandpa had cleaned his glasses,
he reached for the recipe book.
"Now, two cups of **carrots**.

Yummy! Let's start digging..."

Jenny looked around the garden.
"How funny having vegetables in a cake!
Imagine a brussels sprout cake...or a cabbage cake!"
"No, thank you!" laughed Grandpa. "I'll stick to carrot cake any day—
and ours is going to be the tastiest cake ever!"

Grandpa and Jenny washed the carrots
and added them to the cake mix, but...

OH, NO! They
forgot to grate them!
"Oh, dear," said Jenny. "I don't think this looks right."
"We haven't stirred it yet!" said Grandpa.
Jenny stirred and stirred.

"Next," said Grandpa, "we need **walnuts**,
then **eggs** and **sugar**,
and a teaspoon of **cinnamon**."

"Walnuts first…"

OH, NO!
They went in whole!

"Eggs next…"

OH, NO!
Shells and all!

"Here's the sugar…"

OH, NO!
Grandpa reached for
the salt!

"Can't *see* anything
wrong with that now,"
said Grandpa. "Can you?"

With Grandpa's help, Jenny
poured the cake mix into two pans
and then watched as Grandpa
put them carefully into the oven.

Jenny couldn't wait for the cake to bake.
Mommy was going to love it!

Finally the cake was done.
"OH, NO!" said Jenny. "It doesn't look right!"
They each tried a crumb.
"OH, NO!" said Grandpa. "It doesn't taste right!
But we followed the recipe EXACTLY..."

"We forgot the cinna-whatsit, that's why!" cried Jenny.
"And Mommy will be back any minute!

QUICK! Let's hide the cake...

"in the backyard!"

When Mommy came in, Jenny was quiet.
"What's wrong, Jenny?" asked Mommy.
"We were making a birthday surprise for you,"
said Jenny. "But it's a

catastrophe!"

And she led Mommy
out to the backyard. . .

which was full of
beautiful birds!

"You've invited the birds—what a great idea!"
said Mommy. "This is the
best birthday surprise EVER!"

Jenny and Grandpa exchanged a secret smile.
"And I've made a surprise for you too," said Mommy.
"Can you guess what it is?"

"It's a carrot cake!"

cried Jenny.
"It's a good thing we gave ours to
the birds," Grandpa whispered.

"Who wants a piece?" asked Mommy.
"I do!" cried Jenny and Grandpa.
"Happy birthday!"